The Adventures of Logan & Bailey:

Lost in the Woods

by

Jill Paxton

DORRANCE
PUBLISHING CO
EST. 1920
PITTSBURGH, PENNSYLVANIA 15238

Dorrance Publishing Co
585 Alpha Drive
Pittsburgh, PA 15238
Visit our website at *www.dorrancebookstore.com*

ISBN: 978-1-6495-7232-5
eISBN: 978-1-6495-7740-5

The Adventures of
Logan & Bailey:

Lost in the Woods

Chapter 1

Head down, Logan shuffled into the kitchen. Today was the first day in the new house his mom and dad bought.

"Why did Mom make me wear all new clothes to meet the realtor for the new house this morning," he thought.

Looking up he saw a box on the kitchen counter with his name on it. He rummaged through it and pulled out his dog Bailey's leash and laid it aside. Next he discovered one of his favorite T-shirts. It was blue and had his favorite superhero on it. Logan slipped off his new dress shirt and pulled the well-worn T-shirt over his head. Wearing it made him feel a little better.

Noticing the door to the back yard for the first time, Logan pushed it open and trudged down the back steps.

He surveyed the sloping backyard and thought to himself, "Why did we have to move? I am eight-years-old. My friends are at my old school. I don't know anyone here."

Logan's thoughts were interrupted as Bailey came bouncing down the stairs. He brushed past Logan and raced into the sloping yard. Logan laughed as his energetic rat terrier and best friend ran circles in the yard. Moving into the yard, Logan clapped his hands as Bailey raced past. Each circle the dog ran seemed to grow closer to the backside of the unfenced yard.

The backside of the yard had a small bubbling creek with a rock lined water fall. The tall trees on the other side of the creek marked the start of a national park.

Logan knew Bailey should be on a leash in the unfenced yard. As Bailey circled again, a rabbit popped it's head out from behind a bush. The frightened bunny took one look at Bailey and began a terrified zig zagging run across the bottom of the yard. The rabbit was headed for the rocks across the top of the waterfall and the safety of the woods behind it. Logan thought of the dog leash still lying on the kitchen counter as he watched his best friend bound through the water and into the woods after the rabbit.

Afraid for Bailey's safety and of getting in trouble with his parents for not having a leash, Logan raced down the hill after his dog. He waded through the creek. The cold water surrounded his feet as the mud pulled off one of his new shoes. Logan bent down and wrestled the wet, muddy shoe from the creek bottom.

Hopping up and down as he tried to put the shoe back on, Logan fell backwards, landing in a sitting position in the mud.

"Shoot. It is slimy and cold," he grumbled as he flicked the mud off his hands.

Once he had the soggy shoe back on, he stood up and raced into the woods after his dog.

Logan kept moving through the trees, calling, "Bailey, Bailey. Come, come here."

Sometimes he could see Bailey across a clearing. Other times he could hear him barking or breaking through the bushes. Logan kept following him by sight and sound. He didn't pay attention to where they were or what was around him.

Chapter 2

Logan ran and called for Bailey until out of breath, he stopped and listened for his dog. He knew he was going to be in trouble. He should have put Bailey on a leash before going outside. He should not have run through the creek in his new shoes or allowed the sticker bushes to tear holes in his new pants. His parents were going to be so mad.

"What should I do?" he thought to himself. "What would a superhero do?"

Logan was sure that a hero would first catch Bailey. He belonged to Logan. Logan should protect him. He had to be Bailey's super hero.

"Bailey, Bailey, come here. Come, Bailey."

Turning around he could not see anything moving. There was a loud cracking sound. Then there was another one. They were followed by more rustling in the bushes off to his left.

Logan thought he could hear his heart pounding. "What's moving through the bushes? Was it a big animal or a small one?

Could it be Bailey? Could it be a mountain lion or coyotes? Did they have mountain lions and coyotes here? I just moved here. I don't know."

He froze, still as a statue, using his ears to track the wildlife sounds around him. He was off the path where the bushes grew dense under the tall trees. Even the sounds of the birds grew quiet.

He could smell the damp leaves nearby. The branches of the nearby bushes began to shiver, and their leaves began to shake. Logan didn't know if he should run or stay still. He held his breath, closed his eyes, and listened.

Out from under a nearby bush burst Bailey. He was wet, muddy, and delighted to find Logan. His white, brown, and black coat appeared all one color: dirty brown. His short hair was usually smooth with dense, shiny fur. Now he was covered in mud from the white star on his face to the tip of his short tail. His hair was matted with stickers. Logan's dad called them hitchhikers. Logan didn't know if he should hug Bailey or discipline him for running away. Relief that they were together won out. Logan kneeled down. He held his dog for a moment while Bailey happily licked his face. Holding Bailey Logan slipped off his belt and threaded it through Bailey's collar. Now he had him on a makeshift leash. He was not going to let him go again.

Chapter 3

Logan slowly stood up. He clasped the belt leash as Bailey squirmed around and between his legs.

"Now to find our way home," he stated to Bailey.

Logan felt better about the woods now that he was with Bailey. He breathed a sigh of relief. For the first time, he noticed the sun's rays coming through the branches of the trees. He was amazed at how it brought out the many different colors of green that covered the woods.

Once again he thought of superheroes. Now that the dog was saved, what would a superhero do? Would they swing to the top of the highest tree and look around? Logan looked around for a tree to climb. As he gazed skyward at the tall trees, he realized it might be a long fall. Besides how would he tie up Bailey with his small belt? It would not tie around a tree or hold Bailey while Logan tried to climb.

Logan observed the woods around him. He noticed the small purple flowers mixed in with the green of the grass. Looking up he watched two squirrels playing tag among the high branches. They would leap from branch to branch, grab a nut, and then disappear into their nest of leaves. The woods were not so scary. All the trees did not look alike. He tried to make himself remember them. It would help him find his way home. He wondered if his parents were worried about them.

Bailey began to bark at something rustling in the bushes. Whatever animal made the sounds scurried away into the underbrush.

"Ok," Logan sighed. "Bailey, maybe the animals in the woods are more scared of us than we are of them. If we hear a noise, maybe the best thing to do is answer a noise with a noise. You love to bark. Keep it up, boy." Logan exhaled. He felt safe.

Logan scratched Bailey's ears for barking to protect them. His hand was now filthy, so he wiped it on his pants.

Lost in thought, he shared with Bailey, "Mom and Dad will be very angry with us. I am sure we will be in trouble. Maybe it would be better if we didn't go home. If we don't go home, what will we do? I was glad when you came back. I didn't punish you. Maybe they won't be mad at us."

After walking side by side for a while, Logan said, "I am hungry. Are you hungry? I have some candy in my pocket. Do you want one?"

As Logan reached into his pocket. He could feel the clammy candy pieces sticking together. Other pieces were attached to the inside of his pocket.

Separating the sticky candy pieces from each other and his pocket, Logan said, "I know Mom and Dad say not to feed candy to a dog. Maybe it is ok to share if we are lost in the woods."

As they passed a meadow, Logan wondered what nuts or berries he could find to eat if he got really, really hungry.

"Bailey," he asked, "do you think we could eat nuts or berries? It's probably better to just eat what we know is safe. Let's stick with the candy."

Somehow talking to Bailey and sharing his candy comforted Logan. He continued to talk with Bailey as he made his way through the bushes towards a small clearing.

"Did you hear that noise, Bailey? What do you think it is? Will you bark at a bunny this time instead of chasing it? All I need is for you to take off on another rabbit hunt." He laughed. It helped to give the noises he feared a name. He was relieved it was a bunny, not a bear.

When he reached the clearing, Logan noticed piles of rocks stacked in a long line. Someone built a stone wall. Logan decided to use the stones and rocks to spell out HELP. He thought if someone came into the clearing looking for him, it might help them find him.

He reached down to pick up a rock from the pile. A quiet hissing sound followed by a soft rattling noise made Logan jump back from the rocks. Bailey lunged against his leash, barking. Curled up sunning on the rocks was a brown snake with V-shaped crossbar markings. Its wide head with a narrow neck was raising up. It's yellow eyes with long, thin pupils were fastened on Bailey. Logan heard

the hissing and rattling sounds again. He jerked Baily over backwards just as the snake struck out, missing the dog.

Logan dragged Bailey away from the pile of rocks. He did not stay to spell help. He decided that later he might use sticks to create an arrow pointing in the direction he planned to go.

Chapter 4

Logan was relieved they were both safe. He decided to pay better attention. Superheroes would not allow their dog to be bitten by a rattlesnake.

Logan's eyes searched the nearby area. There were two deer in the tall grass. The biggest one raised her head and watched them move. Alerted, both the doe and the fawn raised their white tails and bounded away. Smiling Logan realized he was becoming more comfortable in the woods.

The sun began to drop down on his left. Knowing the sun set in the west, he decided to keep walking toward the sun. He had no idea if home was to the west, but at least he knew he was not wandering in circles.

Bailey began to pant. It felt like hours since they left home. Logan guessed Bailey was thirsty. He listened for water sounds. The first water sounds he heard were squish, squash, squish from the water in his new shoes.

"Oh, man, Mom's going to kill me," he thought. "She was so proud of these shoes. This will not be good. I wonder what she's doing now. Maybe she's unpacking boxes. I don't like this

house, but with Mom and Dad there, it will feel like home. Maybe moving to a new house won't be as bad as I thought."

For a while, the only sounds he heard were the birds in the trees. He loved the cooing of the dove. When he first heard the noise, he wondered if it was his imagination. No, he was sure he heard water. Slowly but surely, still following the setting sun, he found the fast moving stream.

"Let's get you a drink, buddy," said Logan.

As they started down the bank toward the water, Logan's shoes began to slide. He couldn't save himself. He fell backwards and then rolled onto his side. As he struggled to get up, he held tightly to Bailey's leash. He did not want either of them to fall into the water.

"Let's look for a different place to drink. I want to find a place that is safer for both of us," he said to Bailey.

The morning dew had long since dried off the leaves. The warm sun highlighted a small trickle of water bubbling from the rocks above them. Logan squatted down. He and watched Bailey lap the water as it ran down from the rocks trickling into the stream.

Where the rocks met the stream, Logan noticed a small dirt path winding its way up the hill.

"It is probably a path made by the deer," he told Bailey as he pointed towards the hoof prints. "Let's follow it."

The path wound up through the rocks to the top of a hill. When they reached the cliff at the top, Logan peered out over the trees, swamp, and meadow area below him.

"If I just knew which way was home." His wistful voice carried to Bailey.

Suddenly voices carried up the cliff. Logan could not be sure who it was or exactly what they said. He remembered he should be careful around strangers. Ducking down behind a fallen tree, he held Bailey tight against his chest.

Chapter 5

The voices got closer. Logan could tell one was a man. The other voice was higher. It could be a girl or a boy.

"Should we show ourselves, Bailey?" he whispered.

Bailey squirmed out of Logan's hands and jumped up, barking at the intruders. With Bailey bouncing up and down barking, Logan uncurled from his hiding place.

"Well, hello there," said the park ranger standing tall in his uniform. "Are you Logan Williams?"

The man in front of him wore a hat with a flat brim, hiking boots, and had the National Park Service symbol on the sleeve of his grey shirt.

Logan nodded while holding tight to barking Bailey. His eyes rested on the badge above the left pocket of the man's shirt. He looked up when the ranger spoke again.

"We have been looking for you. Your parents are worried. They called our office and asked if we could search for you." Looking at Logan's torn pants, muddy shirt, and squishy shoes, he continued, "It looks like you had quite an adventure. My name is Ranger Rodriguez. This is my son Carlos. Are you up for a walk down the hill to my truck?"

"Yes, thank you," Logan quietly responded. "I have been lost in the woods. I ran after Bailey, he's my dog, when he chased a rabbit."

Ranger Rodriguez motioned towards the trail. They turned and started back down the trail the Ranger and his son came up,

"Your dog looks like he was dipped in fuzzy chocolate. I bet under all that mud he's a great-looking dog," said Carlos. "Where are you from?"

"I guess I am from here now," Logan stated. "We just moved in today."

As they walked down the hill to the ranger's truck. Ranger Rodriguez called his office reporting he found Logan and his dog.

"Let his parents know, they are both unhurt," he added.

When he hung up, he quietly followed behind the boys, letting them talk. They were close to the same age. He could tell they had a lot in common and would become friends.

Waiting by the ranger's truck were Logan's parents. His dad was leaning against his car with his arms crossed.

His mother ran over and hugged him, saying, "We were so worried. Are you ok?"

Logan's face lit up as she hugged him. His words tumbled out as he began to tell them everything that happened.

Ranger Rodriguez listened intently and said, "Logan, you did so many things right when you were lost. Your parents should be very proud of you."

With her hand resting on his shoulder, Logan's mom smiled and stroked his hair.

His dad stepped away from the car and said, "Next time you go out, put a leash on that dog."

"Dad," Logan called, "could we build a fence for our new back yard?"

Walking over to Logan, his dad ruffled his hair as he said, "You bet. But no more rabbit hunting," as they all watched a bunny dash across the road.

This book is dedicated to my grandson Jett and Rudy, his Rat Terrier who helped his parents, Kyle and Emily, raise Jett. Together they helped Jett learn about animals and decisions. Your family is my inspiration.

I would also like to thank my daughter Shannon for her advice; you are my rock and my heart.

Thank you, Mykyta Harets of Neeks Art for the illustrations.

Check out the next book in the Adventures of Logan and Bailey. Logan and Bailey find a baby Raccoon.

Jill C. Paxton

CPSIA information can be obtained
at www.ICGtesting.com
Printed in the USA
BVHW061320210721
612526BV00002BA/4

9 781649 572325